rista F.

Please Write...
I Need Your Help!

Other books by Carol Beach York:

Apple Books:

Secrets in the Attic
When Midnight Comes . . .
The Witch Lady Mystery

Little Apple Books:

The Girls of the
Good Day Orphanage Series:
    Christmas Dolls
    Good Charlotte
    Kate Be Late
    Ten O'Clock Club

Please Write...
I Need Your Help!

Carol Beach York

SCHOLASTIC INC.
New York Toronto London Auckland Sydney

No part of this publication may be reproduced in whole or in part, or stored in a retrieval system, or transmitted in any form or by any means electronic, mechanical, photocopying, recording, or otherwise, without written permission of the publisher. For information regarding permission, write to Scholastic Inc., 730 Broadway, New York, NY 10003.

ISBN 0-590-46842-1

12 11 10 9 8 7 6 5 4 3 2 1   3 4 5 6 7 8/9

Printed in the U.S.A.   28

First Scholastic printing, October, 1993

To my sister Gloria,
with love

1

The first letter from Erin came on a snowy day early in December.

It was waiting for Dorrie when she came home after school. She was later than usual because she stopped by the library. All day the letter was on the table in the front hall, waiting for her as the hours passed.

The winter afternoons were short. By five o'clock the streets were dark. Curtains were drawn at lighted windows, children were called in from play. Dorrie had the sidewalk to herself as she walked along in the falling snow. She liked the snow and the feeling of the library books in her arms.

She was a small girl with light brown hair and freckles. Not the prettiest girl in Miss Johnson's sixth-grade class; that was Rebecca Morey. And not the smartest; math was her downfall.

Dorrie took the letter upstairs to her room and piled her books in a heap on a chair. Her room was the only room on the third floor of the house, and that made it special. Most of the third floor was an attic. There was only this one small bedroom with a slanting ceiling and two windows that looked a long way down to the front yard. Her little brother Stevie said she had all the luck, to have this room.

Sometimes Dorrie thought about people driving by on dark nights, seeing the light shining in her room at the top of the house. She wished she herself could be driving by and see it. Her light must look mysterious, she thought. People would wonder to themselves, "Who is up there at the top of the house in that little room?"

Dorrie stared at the letter in her hand. She was rather surprised to be getting a letter from Erin Lang. They had not been special friends.

Erin had been a timid girl at school, always sort of hovering on the outside of things. Last spring her father had died in an automobile accident. Erin was not in school for a week, and then she came back. Everybody felt uncomfortable around her. Nobody knew what to say. "I'm sorry about your father" — that was about all there was to say.

Mr. Lang taught English literature at the junior college, and had written several books. Dorrie had seen his books in the library. *Shakespeare Country* and *The Reader as Traveler* were two. His picture was on the back flap of the book jacket, along with the usual short book-jacket biography of his life and writing.

After Erin came back to school that spring there were only a few more weeks of classes. Then summer vacation began and Dorrie hardly ever saw Erin. Once she had seen her at the shopping mall with her mother, a slender, dark-haired woman who looked like Erin.

When school started in the fall, Dorrie and Erin were in Miss Johnson's room. At Halloween Dorrie had a party and invited Erin because she was sorry that her father had died. Erin came to the party as a clown, with baggy pants and a white face. Two teardrops were painted on her cheeks.

She took the party invitation as a sign of friendship.

"We're going to move away," she told Dorrie. "I'll write to you."

When Dorrie told her mother about Erin moving away, Mrs. Foster said that wasn't so surprising. "It must be sad for them to stay on in their house, with the memories of Erin's father," she said.

"Would we have to move away if Daddy died?" Stevie had asked uneasily.

"Nobody is going to die," Mrs. Foster said.

Even so, Dorrie thought about it. About having to move away to a strange place, to a new house, to a new room. It was scary to think about.

Erin wasn't exactly moving to a new house, not a house of her own.

"We're going to live with my mom's aunt for a while," she told Dorrie. "Until my mom decides what she wants to do."

And now a letter had come from Erin.

The writing was small and neat — like Erin.

> Aunt Margaret's house is nice. It's bigger than our house was. There are eight rooms and two fireplaces. Aunt Margaret says she is lonely and she's glad we are here.
>
> Mrs. Higgins comes every day to clean and cook. She consults the stars before she does anything. It is her horoscope and she finds it in the paper every day. My mom says this is silly. What do you think?
>
> I looked at Mrs. Higgins' newspaper last week and it said for me, "This is a time to be cautious about money matters and travel plans."
>
> I go to Whittier School. My teacher is Mrs. Gray. I have to walk five blocks. I don't mind that so much. But I miss you and everybody and Miss Johnson.

At the end of the letter Erin gave her phone number, and address:

1136 Riverwood Drive
Ashford — Michigan 00122

Dorrie meant to answer, but the days slipped by. . . .

2

At 1136 Riverwood Drive, Erin waited hopefully for a letter from Dorrie.

She had liked Dorrie best of all the girls at school, and she was sure a letter would come.

When nothing came all week, Erin thought Saturday would be the day. Aunt Margaret said the mail always came about eleven o'clock, and Erin was downstairs waiting long before then.

The night before, she and her mother had spread out the five hundred pieces of a jigsaw puzzle on a table by the living room window. They didn't get very far with it that night, and they went back to it Saturday morning. It was a perfect place for Erin to watch for the letter carrier. While her mother murmured to herself, "Now here's an orange piece — it must go in this corner somewhere," Erin could look out of the window down Riverwood Drive to see if the letter carrier was coming. It was nearly eleven o'clock.

Graceful houses stood behind spacious lawns,

bleak now in the cold December morning. Occasionally a car passed. A delivery van from a florist shop went by.

"You're not trying, Erin," Mrs. Lang scolded playfully.

"Yes, I am."

Aunt Margaret was upstairs. Mrs. Higgins was in the kitchen. The house was quiet with the stillness of a midwinter morning.

Erin tried to give her attention to the puzzle. She pretended that if she didn't watch the street, the letter carrier would come sooner. When the doorbell rang, Erin's mother went to answer, and Erin hurried along with her in case it was her letter arriving.

Instead, a strange man stood outside. He was a tall man in a sheepskin jacket with the collar turned up against the cold. His hair was ruffled by the wind and he was just lifting a hand to smooth it when Erin's mother opened the door.

"Mrs. Lang?" Then he said, "You'll never guess who I am."

The man smiled at Erin's mother.

It was a strange beginning to a conversation. Erin looked at her mother. Was her mother going to be able to guess who this was?

"I'm afraid I — " Mrs. Lang began; the man interrupted her, laughing.

"I didn't think you could," he said. "I'm an old friend of your husband's. Old school chum, to be exact. My name is John Jarvis. I was sorry to hear about Philip. I heard that you were here in Ashford and I wanted to express my sympathies."

He held out his hand to complete the introduction with a handshake.

After that it seemed impolite to let him stand outside in the cold.

He was invited into the living room, and when Aunt Margaret came downstairs a short time later, Mr. Jarvis was sitting in a comfortable chair by the fireside and his whole story was known.

His sheepskin coat — very expensive — lay casually across the sofa arm as though it belonged there; and Erin had even forgotten the letter carrier for a while as she listened to Mr. Jarvis and her mother talking.

"Auntie — " Erin's mother saw Aunt Margaret first and beckoned her toward their little group by the fireplace. "You'll never guess who this is."

Erin laughed then, because that was just what Mr. Jarvis had said. Mr. Jarvis laughed, too. He stood up, tilting his head to Aunt Margaret. A perfect gentleman.

There was a confused expression on Aunt Margaret's gentle face. "Should I know, dear?" she asked.

"Not really," Erin's mother said. "I was teasing. Mr. Jarvis is an old school friend of Philip's. They were in college together. Mr. Jarvis was part of the group on that trip to Australia Philip took in his junior year. Oh, it's so nice to meet one of Philip's friends."

"We lost touch over the years," Mr. Jarvis said apologetically. "It seems a shame, but that so often happens. After college I came here to Ashford and got my antique business started."

"Oh, antiques," Aunt Margaret murmured with approval. She settled herself on the sofa and regarded Mr. Jarvis with interest.

"Anyway, since then I've lost touch with all the fellows from school."

"Yes," Erin's mother said, "I know how that happens."

"I did know that Philip had written a book or two and I always meant to look him up again one day. When I saw this in the local paper it took me quite by surprise."

As Erin watched, Mr. Jarvis took a folded square of newspaper from his pocket. Even before he unfolded it and handed it to her mother, Erin knew what it was. It was the write-up that had been in the *Ashford Herald* about her father's death, and her mother coming to Aunt Margaret's.

> *Ashford is pleased to welcome Mrs. Philip Lang, widow of the author and teacher who died last May in an automobile accident.*
>
> *Lang was the author of several books*

*combining English literature with his
travels in England. He was head of the
English department at Breming College in Breming, Ohio, at the time of
his death.*

 *With Mrs. Lang is her daughter,
Erin. They will be staying with Mrs.
Lang's aunt, Miss Margaret Wilton, of
1136 Riverwood Drive.*

Mrs. Higgins came just then, and spoke aside to Aunt Margaret about lunch arrangements, as she saw there was a visitor.

"Please do stay for lunch, Mr. Jarvis," Aunt Margaret said, but he shook his head.

"Thank you, I have business to attend to at my shop. I was in the vicinity this morning and thought it would be a good time to give my condolences to Philip's wife. But I must be on my way now."

Everybody was standing then, as Mr. Jarvis took up his coat and scarf.

"It was kind of you to stop by," Aunt Margaret said.

"Yes, very kind of you," Erin's mother said.

There was a general movement toward the front door, and Mrs. Higgins disappeared back down the hallway to the kitchen.

At the front door, just as he was going out, Mr. Jarvis turned.

"I've just had a thought," he said. "I can't accept your kind invitation for lunch, but perhaps you would all be my guests for dinner tonight."

He was looking particularly at Erin's mother, but then he turned and smiled at Aunt Margaret and Erin.

Erin's mother glanced at Aunt Margaret. "I must decline," Aunt Margaret said. There was a touch of regret in her voice. "This is a bridge night for me."

Mr. Jarvis looked back at Erin's mother. "Now don't disappoint me," he said, smiling. "Don't tell me you're a bridge player, too."

"Well, no," Mrs. Lang said uncertainly.

"You should go, Carolyn," Aunt Margaret said. "It would do you good to get out."

"Seven o'clock?" Mr. Jarvis suggested.

"All right . . . thank you. Erin and I would enjoy it."

There was just a moment's hesitation before Mr. Jarvis turned and smiled at Erin. As he smiled at her he didn't seem quite as nice as she had thought he was.

"Yes, of course," he said, "Erin."

3

The letter carrier finally arrived just after Mr. Jarvis left, but there was no letter from Dorrie Foster.

On Sunday afternoon Erin wrote another letter herself. She told Dorrie more about the Whittier School. She had been going to it for three weeks now, but she hadn't made any special friends — or friend. Erin thought about this as she wrote. It seemed that one special friend would be enough, a best friend; but she was shy. Because she had joined the class so long after school started, all the girls already had best friends. No one really needed Erin.

> *Aunt Margaret says I can invite my friends here anytime, but I don't know who to invite. Everybody already has their own friends. Maybe I'll get a puppy or a kitten. I told my mom that's what I want for Christmas. She*

12

*said maybe someday. I bet she wants
to surprise me at Christmas.*

*A man who used to go to school with
my father came to see us yesterday
and took us out to dinner. Aunt Margaret couldn't go because she plays
bridge. She loves bridge and never
misses.*

*We went to a Chinese restaurant and
our waitress was Chinese. My mother
said Chinese women are very beautiful, and Mr. Jarvis said my mother
was the most beautiful woman in the
restaurant. Then he said well maybe it
was me — the most beautiful woman.
But he just said that. He winked at my
mother when he said it, so I know he
didn't really mean it.*

Erin thought that was about all she had to write
to Dorrie for this letter. She signed her name, still
thinking about dinner at the Chinese restaurant.
It had not been fun, somehow.

She added a P.S.

*I don't think Mr. Jarvis really
wanted me to come along.*

Then she wrote another P.S.

13

Please write — you are my only friend.

Dorrie found Erin's second letter on the hall table when she came home from school a few days later. But she couldn't read it right away. She had hurried home, bringing her friends Jane Ann and Patsy with her. Dorrie's mother had promised to drive them to the mall after school. They were going to start their Christmas shopping!

Jane Ann was a thin girl with braces on her teeth and long yellow hair she said she was never going to cut in her whole life.

Patsy had red hair, and was likely to jump around and giggle when she got excited about something. She was excited about going to the mall and she was already telling Dorrie all the things she wanted to buy.

"My mom wants perfume — the kind that sprays out, you know. And I'm going to get earrings for my sister and I can wear them sometimes. . . ."

They entered the house still talking when suddenly Stevie pushed through shouting, "Monsters from Mars!" He had run ahead to beat them home, and his cap and jacket lay in a heap on the hall bench.

"Hello, girls." Mrs. Foster came down the stairway. "All set for the mall? Get your jacket on, Stevie, and come along while I drive them."

14

"I can stay here — I'm big enough."

"No, you can't stay here. Now get your jacket on."

"I'm big enough — I can watch TV — "

Stevie's pleas were no use. He put on his jacket, grumbling to himself. Patsy took his hat and hid it behind her back. Jane Ann admired her hair in the hall mirror. Dorrie ran upstairs at the last minute because she wanted to wear her silver bracelet, and she had forgotten until just that moment.

"Now is everybody *ready*?" Mrs. Foster said hopefully.

They all went out to the car and juggled around for places to sit while Mrs. Foster shivered and said, "Why does it take cars so long to heat up!"

"Not in the summer," Stevie shouted. Patsy giggled and Dorrie poked Stevie with her elbow.

Then they were on their way.

The mall was already wondrously decorated for Christmas. Some decorations had been put up even before Thanksgiving. "Earlier and earlier every year," Dorrie's father had said.

There was a big sign at the mall entrance:

18 SHOPPING DAYS TILL CHRISTMAS

Shoppers were everywhere. The brightly lighted shops were filled with good cheer, the murmur of voices, a few million small children.

"Rudolph the Red-Nosed Reindeer" was playing on a loudspeaker.

Mrs. Foster said she would be back at exactly eight o'clock, and drove off with Stevie.

"I could have stayed home. I could have watched TV."

The girls' shopping was a great success. At seven o'clock, rustling with packages, they settled into a booth at The Pizza Pan.

"For my sister." Patsy opened a small bag and held earrings up to her own ears.

Dorrie had bought a video of *Treasure Island* for Stevie and a Beauty Kit for her mother. The kit had bubble bath, bath oil, bath powder, and pink perfumed soap. She had bought pretty blue stationery for Grandma Foster and Miss Johnson at school.

There were still gifts to buy, but there would be other shopping days.

Dorrie felt perfectly and completely happy as she drank her root beer and ate pizza.

When they left the mall, a man was up on a ladder by the sign changing the 18 to 17. Another shopping day was gone.

The parking lot was not as crowded as it had been when they first came. There were some empty places now, but shopping would go on until the stores closed at nine.

Dorrie and Jane Ann and Patsy stood by the

entrance, gripping their bags of gifts and stamping their feet to keep warm. The cold had been increasing all day. The sky was clear above, and the wind was sharp. Dorrie was the first one to see the car coming. Her father was driving. It was warm inside the car; no waiting this time. And as they drove home, other car lights were shining out of the darkness around them.

This is a wonderful day, Dorrie thought, hugging her packages. She had found just exactly what she wanted for Stevie and her mother and Miss Johnson and Grandma Foster . . . and the mall was so beautiful with the Christmas trees and the music. . . .

When I get home I'll hide the presents, Dorrie thought. Christmas seemed so close and yet still so far away. It was hard to wait.

At home, she hid the presents first thing. At the very back of her closet. Then at last, before she went to bed, she had a chance to read the second letter from Erin. The letter made her feel sad. Some of the fun of the trip to the mall faded away as she read the letter.

She had had such a good time all day. Even at school she had had a good time, planning the trip to the mall with Jane Ann and Patsy, looking forward to it.

But Erin had no friends to invite home after school. She had no one to go to the mall with, to shop and eat pizza with.

Patsy with her giggles and Jane Ann with her long yellow hair seemed to look over Dorrie's shoulder as she read the letter from Erin.

She was high up in her room. Her special room. But even here on the top floor, she could hear the sounds of the piano from the living room below. Stevie was banging out "Jingle Bells." At nine o'clock, like a store closing at the mall, Stevie would be closed up and headed for bed.

But he was still downstairs now, for a last few minutes.

"Jingle bells, jingle bells, jingle all the way — " Stevie sang along as he played.

Dorrie came to the end of the letter.

> *Please write — you are my only friend.*

Dorrie couldn't ignore that.

She took a sheet of notebook paper and began:

Dear Erin,

But that was as far as she got. She wanted to write something happy and cheerful, something to cheer up Erin far away in Michigan at a new school where everybody already had their own friends.

But she didn't really know Erin very well. She

18

"I'm good at jigsaws," Erin said. "We had one once with a thousand pieces."

Aunt Margaret smiled. Then she said, "Sometimes it's nice for your mother to go out to dinner without a lot of other people tagging along."

"You're not a lot of other people," Erin said.

"Oh," Aunt Margaret said, "sometimes even one other person is one too many — why, listen, I think I hear your mother now. She's back early."

There was a brief murmur of voices, the closing of the front door, and then Erin's mother came into the living room. She looked bright and happy, already beginning to draw off her gloves.

"John couldn't come in," she said. It was always "John" nowadays, not "Mr. Jarvis" anymore. Erin wasn't sure exactly when this change of name had taken place.

"I was hoping to see him." Aunt Margaret sat back in her chair and gave up on the puzzle for the evening. "He's such a charming man."

Erin's mother tossed her purse on a chair and unbuttoned her coat. "He has a business appointment tomorrow morning in West Shore. It's a long drive for him, but he's excited about some cabinet he hopes to get for his shop — and by the way, he wants us all to come and visit his shop Saturday."

"Even me?" Erin asked.

"Of course you, sweetie," her mother said. "That's why he made it Saturday."

Two weeks of Christmas vacation were coming up, but Mr. Jarvis probably hadn't thought of that. Erin didn't particularly want to see his shop; but if she had to go, Saturday was as good a time as any.

Saturday came. The skies were overcast — low and white; there would surely be snow before the day's end.

Aunt Margaret wore a heavy, long coat and a thick velvet hat pulled down close around her face. She feared colds in winter months. At two o'clock Erin was given the job of watching for Mr. Jarvis' car, while her mother adjusted her coat collar and hat and scarf carefully at the hall mirror.

"I told John to just tap the horn and we'd be right out," she said, arranging her scarf another way entirely and choosing a different pair of gloves.

It seemed to Erin a lot of fuss just to go and look at some old furniture and stuff from long ago.

When Mr. Jarvis came they were all soon tucked into the car — with special consideration to Aunt Margaret's comfort and not much to Erin's. "Just slip in there, darling," her mother said, motioning in the general direction of the back seat.

They drove through town and then for a short distance along a winding road in a wooded area.

"It's very beautiful here in the summer," Mr. Jarvis said.

And it was beautiful even now in December, but in a different way. There was a deep silence to the dark, bare trees and the soft white sky already like twilight.

Just beyond the woods they came to the antique shop. It was right at the roadside, with a parking area at the side. An old-fashioned wooden sign creaked on a bracket over the door. JARVIS FINE ANTIQUES was painted in curlique letters, very hard to read. Erin squinted to make out the words.

She was first out of the car, with her mother next, and Mr. Jarvis helping Aunt Margaret with gallant gestures.

"Well, this is it," he said, particularly to Erin's mother. And then they all went inside.

An elderly gentleman came forward to greet them, rising from a small stool near the back of the shop. No one else was there.

"Mr. Arlington," Mr. Jarvis said, "may I introduce these three lovely women. Mrs. Lang, Miss Wilton, Miss Erin."

"So pleased." Mr. Arlington shook hands with everyone, even Erin. Most of his hair was gone, and his smile was lit by several gold teeth. As he shook Erin's hand he gave it an extra pat, as though she was his favorite.

"Mr. Arlington has been with me for several years. Indispensable, indispensable. Knows more about antiques than I do," Mr. Jarvis said.

25

Mr. Arlington shook his head modestly, but he looked pleased.

Aunt Margaret drew off her velvet hat and ran her fingers through her hair to revive it.

"Lovely, charming." Erin's mother began to walk slowly along the row of antiques on display.

There was a steady background sound of clocks ticking, and a smell of furniture polish mingled with a faintly musty odor.

"I keep eucalyptus, or the musty smell would be even stronger," Mr. Jarvis said, motioning toward a copper pot of eucalyptus branches at one side of the shop. "Their spicy odor triumphs to some extent."

"Yes, yes indeed," Mr. Arlington agreed, rubbing his hands together cheerfully.

Through old-fashioned small-paned windows the bleak light of the winter afternoon shone in upon rocking chairs and tables with clawed feet, oil lanterns and framed pictures, glassware, andirons, log buckets, pewter, brass plates, hand-painted china.

Aunt Margaret picked up a wooden box with a metal top and a handle attached. "My grandmother used to have one of these coffee grinders in her kitchen," she said. "My, this brings back memories."

Erin put out her hand and touched a rocking chair arm, gently setting the chair in motion. When she looked up shyly, only Mr. Arlington had noticed, and he nodded and smiled to show it was all right to touch things.

Erin liked the ticking clocks. She would have liked the whole shop well enough if it hadn't been Mr. Jarvis' shop.

And then she broke the flower vase.

She didn't mean to; her elbow knocked against it as she turned in a narrow space between two dark old tables, their surfaces glimmering with shadows.

The vase made a dreadful noise and Mr. Arlington put out his arms — as though to catch it and save it, even at the distance he stood.

"Ohh . . ." Mrs. Lang let out a startled exclamation and swung around to see what had happened. Aunt Margaret put her hand to her mouth with an expression of dismay.

Erin stared down at the shattered glass on the floor at her feet. She felt her face begin to flush and her heart beat faster. When she looked up, the first face she saw was Mr. Jarvis'. It was a face of anger and disgust, an unforgiving face.

"Erin!" Mrs. Lang came toward her.

"I didn't mean to — "

"It's all right, nothing to worry about — accidents will happen." Mr. Jarvis was suddenly his usual smiling self again. He was all smiles. He smiled at Erin and Erin's mother. Even Aunt Margaret got a smile, and Mr. Arlington, who hurried off for a broom to sweep up the pieces.

27

"It's past repair," Mrs. Lang said, stooping beside Erin and taking up one of the fragments. "Oh, John, I'm so sorry."

"It's all right, quite all right." Mr. Jarvis couldn't be nice enough. He drew Mrs. Lang up from the broken glass and put his arm fondly around her shoulders. When had he started doing that? Erin wondered. But she was too distressed and embarrassed to think much about it just then.

The glass was swept up and Mr. Jarvis insisted no one was to worry about the vase. "No indeed, no indeed," Mr. Arlington agreed as he carried off the remains in a dustpan.

But the afternoon was ruined for Erin. She had seen the look on Mr. Jarvis' face, the look of anger before he began to smile again. He wasn't a kind man, like Daddy had been. Daddy would never look so mean and disgusted about something that was an accident. Erin hadn't meant to knock over the vase.

Aunt Margaret said she wanted to buy the coffee grinder that was like her grandmother's and Mr. Jarvis said no, she couldn't buy it. He gave it to her as a gift.

Aunt Margaret was as pleased as she could be. "You're too kind," she told Mr. Jarvis. Erin could tell Aunt Margaret thought he was wonderful.

When they left, the coffee grinder was put on

the back seat of the car between Erin and Aunt Margaret, in her long coat and velvet hat.

Erin's mother sat in front again, with Mr. Jarvis.

They drove back toward town along the same silent winter road. No other customers had come to the shop while they were there, and Erin thought Mr. Arlington must get lonely way out there all by himself.

The snow had not begun yet, but it would surely begin soon.

"Going to snow," Mr. Jarvis said, and Erin's mother turned to him and they smiled at each other.

Only Erin had seen his real face.

5

And now a sad time began for Erin, when it should have been a happy time, Christmas holidays.

A green pine tree was brought into Aunt Margaret's living room and put into a stand by the bay window.

Mrs. Higgins put water in the tree stand, and a sprinkle of sugar in the water. "That keeps it fresh," she said. It was a special Christmas for her because she was six times a grandmother now and had many toys to buy. She read her horoscope every day in the newspaper, and bustled around the kitchen with more energy and good spirits than usual because it was Christmastime.

But it was a sad time for Erin.

More and more often her mother was gone from the house in the evenings, out with Mr. Jarvis. She always seemed to be thinking about him and planning her next meeting with him.

When Erin asked her questions, she answered absently.

When they trimmed the tree, she was thinking of other things.

"Let's put the glass bells near the top; let's put the golden horn here — Mom?" Erin wanted the tree to be perfect.

"Anywhere is fine, sweetie," her mother answered.

"Doesn't the angel look good right in the front?"

"Yes, that's fine, sweetie."

Aunt Margaret helped, putting on silvery icicle strands one by one with a fine patience. She had many beautiful old ornaments that had been in her family when she was a child. "John will love these ornaments," Erin's mother said.

They worked on the decorating into the evening. Mr. Jarvis called at one point and Erin's mother went to talk to him on the telephone; Erin and Aunt Margaret finished the tree alone.

"Now that's the prettiest tree in Ashford," Mrs. Higgins said, when she came the next morning and saw the tree decorated and complete.

Still it was a sad time for Erin. It wasn't like other Christmases had been, when Daddy was alive. "It's their first Christmas without him," she heard Aunt Margaret telling Mrs. Higgins. Aunt Margaret was speaking softly, but Erin overheard. "This first Christmas will be the hardest for them."

Maybe it was a hard Christmas because it was the first . . . but it was more than that. Erin felt her mother was drifting away from her.

"Can we wrap presents today?" she asked her mother one afternoon. They had always done this together, putting everything out on the dining room table — gifts, ribbon, wrapping paper, scissors, sticky tape, gift tags. All afternoon they would wrap and write names on tags. They would take a break and drink cocoa with marshmallows.

But this time her mother said, "Aunt Margaret will help you wrap. I'm going with John this afternoon to look at some things he wants to buy for his shop."

Erin had told Dorrie about the visit to the antique shop and how angry Mr. Jarvis had looked when she broke the vase.

I told my mom he was mad at me
when I broke the vase, but she said it
was my imagination. It wasn't.

Erin underlined "It wasn't." Then she wrote:

I like Aunt Margaret's house, but I
wish we could move away somewhere
where Mr. Jarvis doesn't live.

One morning when her mother was sitting at the writing desk in her room addressing Christmas cards, Erin went in and asked to have a card.

"Of course," Mrs. Lang said. "Choose whichever one you want."

"It's for a girl back home," Erin said.

"Ashford is our home now," her mother said gently. "At least for now, and maybe for always. You like Ashford, don't you?"

"It's all right." Erin kept her eyes on the box of cards. "Are we going to buy a house here?"

Her mother hesitated. "Let's just see what happens, shall we. Now choose your card."

There were two kinds of cards. One had an evergreen tree in a snowy moonlit field, the other had a bright red Christmas table with a roast turkey and candles burning and people sitting round. It was the most happy, and Erin chose that card.

She addressed the envelope to Dorrie, and wrote inside the card:

We have our tree now. I'm still hoping for a puppy or a kitten for Christmas.

She didn't try to tell Dorrie about the sadness she felt. It was a hard thing to write about.

6

As Christmas day grew closer and closer, Erin kept a lookout around the house for signs that a puppy or kitten was hidden somewhere.

She looked with particular care in the kitchen and the basement below. The basement seemed the best place to hide a surprise pet. She looked in Mrs. Higgins' cupboards for hidden cans of cat food or dog food.

There was nothing.

One afternoon when she was helping Mrs. Higgins make Christmas cookies she heard a barking outside and rushed to the kitchen window, but it was only a neighborhood dog chasing a squirrel across the snowy yard. The dog's leash was dragging behind and his owner stood on the sidewalk calling, "Come back here, Freddy. Leave that squirrel alone!"

Erin watched as the dog she had thought might be her own Christmas puppy finally ran back toward the sidewalk. The squirrel escaped up a tree.

"I guess a puppy wouldn't bark that loud," she said with disappointment.

"Puppy?" Mrs. Higgins looked up from the cookies. "What's that about a puppy?"

"Am I getting one for Christmas?" The words rushed out and Erin watched Mrs. Higgins' face hopefully. "Am I? If you tell me, I won't tell. I'll act surprised. I *promise*."

Her voice urged Mrs. Higgins to share the secret.

Mrs. Higgins was only puzzled. "I don't know anything about a puppy," she said doubtfully. She frowned a bit, too; puppies made work and she had enough work already. She didn't need a puppy underfoot all day.

"Maybe it's a kitten," Erin said. "That's just as good."

It *was* just as good, maybe better. Kittens were fluffy and cuddly. When you stroked them you could hear them purr.

"I don't know anything about a kitten, either," Mrs. Higgins said. She flattened the cookie dough with her rolling pin and began cutting star shapes with a cookie cutter. "Here," she said, "don't be looking so unhappy. You make the Christmas trees."

Erin took the Christmas tree cookie cutter with a sigh. It was the only cookie cutter that was green plastic. The others were aluminum. One tree. Two trees. Three trees. She moved the cutter from place to place along the rolled-out dough. Maybe Mrs. Higgins was just good at keeping secrets, she thought. Maybe there really was a puppy or a kitten hidden somewhere, waiting for Christmas morning.

As she pushed her green plastic Christmas tree into the dough, Erin peeked up at Mrs. Higgins. But Mrs. Higgins' plump, ruddy face gave no clues. All her attention was on the cookies.

"I'll probably get a puppy or a kitten," Erin said with determination. "My mom promised."

"Oh, Erin, I didn't *promise*."

The voice from the doorway surprised both Erin and Mrs. Higgins. They had not heard footsteps coming along the hall. Mrs. Lang stood in the doorway.

"I said maybe *someday*, don't you remember, honey." She came into the kitchen and stood by the table where the cookie dough was rolled out and the stars and bells and Christmas trees lay outlined by the cutters, ready to go onto the baking pan. Mrs. Higgins began to scoop them up with a spatula, leaving holes in the dough where they had been.

"You sort of promised."

"I meant someday when we have our own home. It wouldn't be fair to Aunt Margaret to bring a new little puppy or kitten here with all her lovely furniture and drapes and things. You know how puppies are, Erin. They chew up everything and wet on the rugs. And kittens scratch and claw — "

"I wouldn't let it . . . I wouldn't let it bother anything . . . I'd watch it all the time and it would be good."

Erin felt cross and cheated. She didn't have anybody — not even her mother anymore. Now she couldn't even have a puppy or a kitten.

Mrs. Higgins had filled a cookie pan, thumped it onto the oven rack and closed the oven door loudly. She began to move about the kitchen noisily, to remind Mrs. Lang that she was there, listening to what should be a private conversation.

"You couldn't watch it all the time, honey. You'd be at school."

"No I wouldn't, not all the time."

Mrs. Lang sighed.

Mrs. Higgins gave all her interest to something in a far corner of the kitchen.

"We'll have our own home soon. You know staying with Aunt Margaret is just temporary, just until we decide what we want to do."

But Erin tossed the plastic cookie cutter on the table and ran out of the kitchen.

Upstairs in her room, Erin buried her head in her pillow and cried. For so many things. Not having a puppy or a kitten . . . missing Daddy . . . missing her mother.

No one came to coax Erin not to cry.

Mrs. Higgins wouldn't have come, even if kitchen duties permitted. That was not her place.

Aunt Margaret didn't come. She didn't even know Erin was crying.

Erin's mother didn't come. She thought it was better to leave Erin alone, to let Erin realize for herself how unfair it would be to bring a puppy or a kitten into Aunt Margaret's home.

No one came to Erin's room.

By and by it began to grow dusky outside. The winter afternoon was shortening toward evening. In far away Ohio, Dorrie Foster was once again walking home through darkness and falling snow with her armful of library books, while lights shone from the windows along the silent street.

7

In Ashford, the day before Christmas, snow began to fall for the first time in more than a week. Aunt Margaret said that was just as it should be. They would have a white Christmas after all.

A splendid Christmas Eve dinner was in preparation, guests were invited, a Christmas wreath hung outside on the front door.

The afternoon darkened even earlier than usual as the snow continued. In her room, Erin sat in the lamplight at her desk and wrote once more to Dorrie.

> *I'm not getting a puppy or a kitten
> for Christmas. My mom told me. I
> have to wait until we get a house of
> our own.*

Erin bent close over the notepaper. She wanted to write more, to write a long letter like the ones

she had written to Dorrie before. Somehow tonight she couldn't think of anything else to say.
It was Christmas Eve. But it didn't seem like
Christmas Eve. Christmas Eve had always been
so happy.

> *We're having company tonight. Aunt*
> *Margaret's friends. Mr. Jarvis will be*
> *coming. He's always coming. I wish*
> *he'd stay home for once.*
> *He doesn't like me very much. Yes-*
> *terday I went to the post office to get*
> *Aunt Margaret some stamps. I was*
> *walking home and he drove right past*
> *me in his car and didn't even stop and*
> *offer me a ride. I was freezing, and I*
> *know he saw me. He was probably glad*
> *I was freezing.*

Erin chewed the end of her pen. That was about
all she could think of to write.

It was time to go downstairs. Guests would be
arriving.

Mr. Jarvis was the first to arrive.

Erin was kneeling on the floor by the Christmas
tree picking up a few strands of icicles that had
slipped from the tree. When she looked up, there
was Mr. Jarvis in the hall, taking off his coat,
brushing snowflakes from his hair. Then he put

his arm around Erin's mother and they came into the living room.

Aunt Margaret said, "Ah, the first guest."

Erin slipped away into the kitchen. She would rather help Mrs. Higgins than talk to Mr. Jarvis. But she got sent right back into the living room with a tray of fancy crackers decorated with cheese and olives and tiny shrimp. Mrs. Higgins called these "cheese delights."

Mr. Jarvis was still the only guest. Erin's mother and Aunt Margaret sat on a sofa by the fireplace and Aunt Margaret beckoned to Erin. "Put that tray down, Erin, and come help us guess which one is Mr. Jarvis. Your mother has found an old photo album of your father's, from his college days."

"Pictures from the Australian trip are in here somewhere." Erin's mother was turning the pages of the album slowly. Mr. Jarvis stood beside the sofa, looking down at the photographs as they went by.

"Here we are." The pages stopped turning and Mr. Jarvis leaned down for a better look.

"*That's* you," Erin's mother said with a pleased laugh. "I can tell right away, because you're the tallest."

"You've found me." Mr. Jarvis nodded agreeably.

"You had a beard!" Erin's mother laughed again. She turned the album so Erin could see.

41

"We all had beards," Mr. Jarvis said. "We got lazy about shaving in Australia, roughing it, you know."

Four young men were grouped in front of a couple of large tents on a barren stretch of ground. Only a few small trees offered shade. To Erin it looked like a dreary place to be. But it must have been fun for the young men. "Those were great days," Mr. Jarvis was saying.

"There's Daddy," Mrs. Lang reminded Erin, touching her fingertip to one of the small faces in the photo.

"I know," Erin said. She had seen the album pictures before. She didn't want Mr. Jarvis to think she didn't know which one was her own father. He wasn't the tallest in the picture, that was Mr. Jarvis; but Erin thought he was the most handsome.

"Almost twenty-five years ago," Mr. Jarvis said. "That album brings back memories."

Mrs. Lang turned to the next page, and Erin had a glimpse of more pictures of tents and the sandy ground of Australia — and then the doorbell rang to announce guests arriving. While they were still being welcomed in the entryway, another group came along. Some of the people had already met Mrs. Lang and Erin. Some knew Mr. Jarvis, or at least knew of his shop. Ashford was not a large town.

In the living room everyone admired the tree and agreed that a white Christmas was delightful.

The photo album was put aside. Erin took up the tray of Mrs. Higgins' cheese delights and offered them to everyone. The dinner to come could not be surpassed, but the cheese delights were a great success.

One woman stopped Erin for a moment, as she offered the tray. "Margaret tells me you've been to visit Mr. Jarvis' shop. Did your mother like it? She seems to like Mr. Jarvis."

"I'm surprised he still has that shop." A second woman lowered her voice confidentially. "I heard it wasn't doing at all well these days. He's let everyone go except poor Mr. Arlington, and he's probably working for next to nothing."

The first woman put her finger to her lips and shook her head. "Not now, Eleanor," she said softly.

It's because I'm here, Erin thought.

She felt clumsy and self-conscious as she went on past the women with her tray of crackers. Behind her she could hear them still talking in hushed voices. They didn't want her to hear what they were saying about Mr. Jarvis and his antique shop.

Later that night, when the guests were gone and Erin had a chance to be alone with her mother, she told her what the women had said about Mr. Jarvis' antique shop.

Mrs. Lang had come into Erin's room to say good night. She sat on the edge of Erin's bed. She listened to what Erin said and then patted her hand. "I'm sure John's business will be just fine, Erin. It's nothing for you to worry about."

8

Christmas cannot last forever. By and by the beautiful tree was taken down, the ornaments packed away for another year.

School began again and Erin walked the five blocks on cold, snowy days. The girls in her class were friendly to her now, used to her; but she had no special friend.

It was one morning in mid-January, at the breakfast table, that Aunt Margaret said, "Erin ought to see the Winston Park Zoo."

She was glancing over the morning paper as she finished her coffee, and there was a nice little write-up about the zoo.

"It might look like the zoo has settled down for a long winter's nap," Aunt Margaret read from the newspaper, "but it is open the year round and welcomes visitors in every season. Zoos aren't just for summer. For some of the residents, winter is the favorite time of year. Polar bears. Wolves. Seals and penguins. All these enjoy the ice and snow and cold of winter. Come and share a winter day with them."

"Oh, let's go," Erin said. "I've never been to a zoo in the winter." She tried to think how that would be . . . all cold and mysterious, she thought.

"Where is Winston Park?" her mother asked.

"About a half hour's drive," Aunt Margaret said. "The zoo is well worth seeing. It's too much walking for me now, but you two ought to go."

Erin and her mother smiled at each other across the table.

"Let's go," they both said at the same time.

And then Erin's mother added, "John can take us."

Erin was disappointed. She didn't want to go with Mr. Jarvis. Why couldn't she and her mother just go to the zoo together. That would be so much more fun.

"Some Saturday maybe." Her mother was making the plans without asking Erin if she wanted Mr. Jarvis to go with them.

"Or next Friday," Aunt Margaret said. "It's Erin's holiday."

There was a teachers' conference Friday, and no school. Erin had just brought home the news the day before. "You ought to do something special," Aunt Margaret had said when Erin told her. And now there was the zoo.

"Perfect," Mrs. Lang said. "Probably better for

John than Saturday. I'm sure Saturday is busy at the shop."

Erin thought about the shop the Saturday they had visited. It had not been busy. Mr. Arlington was all alone.

No one else seemed to think of that, and arrangements were made for the Friday holiday. Mr. Jarvis was to come at one o'clock.

When the day came the temperature was moderate, for January, and there was a pale sunlight on the snowy lawns of Riverwood Drive. Erin's mother complained of a slight sore throat at breakfast and only wanted fruit juice and coffee.

"That's not enough," Aunt Margaret said. She thought eggs were good for breakfast, or oatmeal with cream; nourishing things. Juice and coffee was not breakfast.

The sore throat did not improve as the morning went on.

By lunchtime it was worse.

"Perhaps you shouldn't go out in the cold, with that throat," Aunt Margaret said. Her face was puckered with concern. She peered closely at Erin's mother. "No breakfast, and now no lunch."

"It hurts to swallow," Mrs. Lang admitted. "And I suppose you're right. I shouldn't go out. But that's no reason Erin and John can't go."

She turned to Erin. "I know you've been looking forward to the zoo, honey."

47

"Not without you." Erin felt a sense of panic. "I don't want to go with Mr. Jarvis *alone*."

"Don't be silly." Her mother smiled, despite her sore throat. "Mr. Jarvis doesn't bite."

"And he has arranged his day for you," Aunt Margaret said. "He'll be coming in just a few minutes."

Erin felt trapped.

She was trapped.

Mr. Jarvis came, promptly at one, and her mother insisted: "You two go along. I want you to."

"I still have at least one lovely lady to escort," Mr. Jarvis said.

Aunt Margaret had said Winston Park was a half hour's drive from Ashford. Mr. Jarvis turned on the car radio and they listened to music and news as they drove along. Even so, it seemed to Erin that the trip lasted forever.

"So you've never been to a zoo in winter?" Mr. Jarvis asked.

"No, we always went in the summer."

Erin looked straight ahead at the highway rushing to meet them. Memories of going to the zoo with her father came back. She had never really forgotten them. He had always liked the polar bears . . . he had bought her hot dogs and popcorn at the refreshment stands. . . .

Days with Daddy at the zoo were far, far away now. And they would never come back again.

Erin looked over at Mr. Jarvis' hands on the steering wheel. He wore soft pigskin gloves. He didn't look poor, she thought, like someone whose shop was failing and who had to let everyone go except Mr. Arlington.

By the time they reached Winston Park the sunlight had faded, the sky was overcast. The parking lot had only a few cars. In the park surrounding the zoo, patches of snow lay in shaded areas. A solitary man was walking a dog near the zoo entrance.

Admission was free. Erin and Mr. Jarvis walked into the zoo through a wide gate, past a sign that said:

WINSTON PARK ZOO
OPEN 7 DAYS A WEEK
8 A.M.– 5 P.M.

Erin had not ever been to this particular zoo, but she knew what zoos were like in summer. Children running around, hot dog stands and ice cream vendors, people strolling on sunny walkways. A little souvenir shop crowded with stuffed animals and posters, trinkets and zoo books. Clusters of people in the lion house at feeding time, while the hungry lions roared and paced their cages. Peanut shells on the walks, balloon men, people sitting on benches in the shade.

Now here, in January, the walks of the Winston Park Zoo were nearly deserted. The refreshment stands were shuttered for the winter, the small vendors gone. There were no bright-colored balloons or places to buy crinkly paper bags of peanuts-in-the-shell.

She walked along with Mr. Jarvis, past closed refreshment stands and empty benches.

The lion house was dim and echoey. No one was there but Erin and Mr. Jarvis.

In the primate house the monkeys sat calmly blinking back at the occasional visitor, grooming themselves and sometimes swinging up on long arms.

There was a small group of people in the elephant building, where there was a baby elephant with its mother.

"This seems to be the main attraction," Mr. Jarvis said.

Erin made her way to the front to see the elephant baby. It stood beside its mother and when she walked a few steps with a slow, lumbering gait, the baby followed along.

The baby had a small baby trunk, and elephant ears, and wrinkled skin, just like its mother. Erin couldn't look at it long enough. She forgot everything else for a few minutes and just stared at the dear baby elephant.

When she turned around at last, she didn't see Mr. Jarvis anywhere. She had thought he was just behind her. Now she couldn't see him anywhere. She was suddenly very much alone. The people who had been beside her were walking away. Their footsteps echoed in the silence. No one else was around.

Erin ran to the doorway and looked out, but Mr. Jarvis was not in sight. The walks of the zoo were bleak-looking in the pale winter light. Where could he be?

She went back toward the monkey house, where they had been last. There were only two boys there and she ran away, back to the deserted paths of the zoo.

All the trees were bare. They looked as abandoned and alone as Erin felt.

Mr. Jarvis was not in the lion house. He was not in the snake house.

The souvenir shop was closed. Not enough people came on winter days to keep the shop open.

Then at last she saw Mr. Jarvis not far away, and she called to him and ran toward him. Surely he could hear her. But he didn't stop to wait for her. He went into a small stone building, but when Erin got there he wasn't there. Gaudy, exotic birds preened their feathers and a zoo maintenance man was hosing down an empty cage.

There was another door at the other end of the building and Erin ran to that. But there was no Mr. Jarvis. Only the deserted walks and the bare trees.

How could she get home, if she couldn't find Mr. Jarvis? Erin began to feel frightened now. Maybe she could find a phone and phone her mother . . . but her mother was sick. Maybe Aunt Margaret would come for her. Aunt Margaret didn't drive . . . but maybe, somehow, she could come and get Erin and take her home.

Erin felt tears in her eyes. A man and woman were walking by, but she couldn't just go up to them and say, "I'm lost." She wasn't exactly lost, anyway. She just couldn't find Mr. Jarvis.

She brushed at the tears and kept her face down so the people wouldn't notice. It wasn't fair that she couldn't find a telephone. She had money, if she could just find a telephone.

"Do you know where there's a telephone?" she asked a woman who looked nice. But the woman didn't know. Around Erin the zoo seemed scary and endless and empty. It was dreadful to be so alone so far from home.

And then she saw Mr. Jarvis again. This time he was sitting on a bench and Erin began to run as hard as she could so he wouldn't get up and go away before she got to him.

Her feet pounded on the asphalt walk, and she arrived beside him flushed and tearful.

"Where were you?" Her voice trembled.

"Waiting here — I knew you'd find me."

"Find you?" Erin was gasping for breath. She brushed the tears back helplessly. She didn't want him to see that she was crying, but he could see.

"We got separated," he said casually. "I knew you'd come here to find me."

"Come here?" Erin looked around, bewildered. She saw that they were by the entrance gate of the zoo. "How could I come here?" she asked. "I didn't know I was supposed to come here. You didn't tell me to come here — "

"Everybody comes back to the entrance of a place if they get separated," Mr. Jarvis said. "Isn't that what you and your mother do?"

Erin stared at him and new tears came into her eyes.

"My mother and I always stay together," she said.

9

At home. Safe at home at last.

There was still light in the sky. Mrs. Higgins was preparing dinner in the kitchen and the lonely walkways of the zoo were far away.

Aunt Margaret sat in the chair she liked by the fireplace. Erin's mother was on the sofa with a shawl around her shoulders. A book she had been reading was set aside on the pillows.

"But darling, you shouldn't have been frightened," she told Erin. "You were bound to find each other."

Aunt Margaret said "Of *course*," as though there could be no doubt. As though there had never been cold, deserted paths by silent zoo buildings, a gray sky overhead, nowhere to turn for help.

"I'd have found her by and by, if she hadn't found me," Mr. Jarvis said cheerfully. "She was just daydreaming at some point and wandered off."

Daydreaming? Wandered off? That wasn't true.

"I was only looking at the elephants," she said. But she knew her mother wasn't really listening. Her mother would listen to Mr. Jarvis. Aunt Margaret would listen to him. The frightening time at the zoo couldn't get into this warm, bright room where the firelight was glowing. Only Erin had known the panic. No one else could share it. No one else even believed it.

Well, maybe there *was* someone who would understand.

When she went up to her room after dinner, Erin wrote to Dorrie. She didn't tell anything about school or any other things this time, just the trip to the zoo.

> *I think he wanted to lose me. I think*
> *he wanted to scare me and make me*
> *afraid.*

As she wrote, the lonely silence of the zoo on a cold winter day seemed to be around her again. The boys in the monkey house had looked big and rough . . . the birds screeched in the bird house . . . the door of the souvenir shop was locked up tight . . . what would she do if Mr. Jarvis drove away in his car and left her there alone?

She was just finishing the letter when Aunt Margaret knocked at her bedroom door.

"Not in bed yet?"

Erin moved her letter to Dorrie toward the back of her desk, hoping Aunt Margaret wouldn't notice.

"No, not yet," she said.

"I'm sorry you had a bad time today," Aunt Margaret said in her kindly way.

"He doesn't like me," Erin blurted out. "He lost me on purpose."

"Oh, Erin, don't say that." Aunt Margaret looked shocked. "Mr. Jarvis would never do anything like that."

"He *did*, he *did*," Erin insisted. "He just went away and left me."

"Erin — " Aunt Margaret held up a hand to stop the rush of words, but Erin didn't stop.

"He doesn't like me. I know he doesn't like me."

"He *does* like you," Aunt Margaret said. "He is very fond of both you and your mother."

"Not me," Erin said. She turned away from Aunt Margaret. Aunt Margaret didn't understand.

Then she felt Aunt Margaret's hand on her shoulder.

"Tomorrow," Aunt Margaret said, "let's the two of us go out and have lunch together. We'll talk about Mr. Jarvis."

Erin didn't answer.

"Come on," Aunt Margaret coaxed, "give me a smile. You'll like the place I have in mind. The chocolate cake has frosting an inch thick."

Erin couldn't help smiling just a little. "An inch thick?"

Aunt Margaret nodded. "That's a promise."

10

The next day, Saturday, was cold. Snow was falling.

"How nice that you and Aunt Margaret are having lunch together," Erin's mother said. Her throat was better; however, she was going to stay in for the day. Erin felt nervous and uncomfortable. She knew Aunt Margaret was going to talk about Mr. Jarvis — and Erin didn't want to.

The restaurant Aunt Margaret had chosen for lunch was called simply "The Tearoom." There was snow flickering at the windows, a low murmur of voices.

The tablecloths were a soft golden color and each table had a single yellow chrysanthemum in a small glass vase.

Ice water arrived, and menus with gold writing on red covers.

There was butter in small china dishes.

They ordered chicken salad and tea for Aunt

Margaret, a grilled cheese sandwich and milk for Erin. And they didn't talk about Mr. Jarvis right away. A woman began to play a piano at the far end of the room, and it was very sweet in the winter day to hear the piano music above the murmur of voices.

It was while they were waiting for dessert that Aunt Margaret began talking about Mr. Jarvis. "When we love people, we want them to be happy," she said, smiling at Erin gently. "Isn't that right?"

Erin moved her head in a sort of nod. "I guess so."

"Of course we do." Aunt Margaret was very sure about this. "And your mother is happy with her new friend, John. You should be happy for her."

She paused.

"Your mother loved your father very much, but her life is lonely now. It's good for her that John has come into her life. If she thought you didn't like John, that would make her very unhappy."

Erin looked down at the table. "Well, I don't like him," she mumbled.

"You must try, dear." Aunt Margaret leaned toward Erin with an urging manner. "For your mother's sake you must try. She would be very sad if she thought you didn't like John."

Erin felt more alone and bereft than ever. Aunt

Margaret was saying she shouldn't tell her mother that she didn't like Mr. Jarvis. She would spoil her mother's happiness.

"You know, Erin, your mother might want to remarry some day," Aunt Margaret said. Her face had a pleased look, as though she thought this would be a good thing to happen.

"Get married to him?" Erin felt her throat tightening, but she had to ask.

Aunt Margaret tilted her head a bit. "Would that be so bad? I think it would make your mother very happy. But she wants you to like John, too."

Erin felt guilty then for not liking Mr. Jarvis, for making her mother unhappy.

Her dessert came — the famous chocolate cake. She poked at it with her fork, hardly caring now. A dreadful future stretched out before her. Mr. Jarvis wouldn't want her around after he married her mother; they would send her far away to some school where the teachers were cruel and she had no friends . . . or worse, they *wouldn't* send her to school. She would have to live at home with Mr. Jarvis. If she went anywhere with him, he would lose her. If she did anything wrong, he would be angry.

Then she remembered the antique shop. She never wanted to go there again. What if Mr. Jarvis and her mother made her work there when she grew up? What if she broke things?

"What about his shop? Will he still have that?"

"The antique shop?" Aunt Margaret was eating her ice cream. A waiter hovered in the background. The woman at the piano began another pretty tune.

"Yes, of course he will keep the shop. Why do you ask?"

Erin stared down at her plate. "No reason," she said.

"I know. You're thinking about what my friends said. Your mother told me. Well, it is true, business hasn't been good. And I think you're old enough to understand, so I'll tell you. I'm going to help John a bit with the business."

Aunt Margaret paused, and then added, "And your mother is enthusiastic about helping out, too, after they — " She paused again.

"After they what?" Erin stared at Aunt Margaret helplessly.

"Well, after they get married, dear."

By and by Aunt Margaret paid the bill and they left the restaurant.

The lady was still playing the piano.

Snow was still falling.

The day was still cold.

Nothing had changed.

And everything had changed.

11

When Dorrie got Erin's letter telling about the day at the zoo, she was puzzled. Would Mr. Jarvis really try to lose Erin on purpose? How horrid that would be. Dorrie felt herself getting mad at Mr. Jarvis.

She was lying on her bed reading the letter, and when she came to the next part she sat up with surprise.

> *Aunt Margaret took me to lunch the next day. She thinks Mr. Jarvis is wonderful and she said I shouldn't say anything to my mother about how I don't like him. She said it would make my mother unhappy. My mom and Aunt Margaret are going to give Mr. Jarvis some money to help out with his shop. I think my mom is going to marry Mr. Jarvis.*

"Oh, *no*," Dorrie said, just as Stevie came to her doorway.

"Who are you talking to?" Stevie stuck his head in and looked around the room.

"Go away." Dorrie frowned at him.

"Go read a book." Stevie stuck out his tongue.

"*Go away.*"

"Mom wants some help in the kitchen." Stevie delivered his message and jumped back down the stairs two at a time.

Dorrie got up slowly and put Erin's letter back in its envelope. She felt more sorry than ever for Erin. First her father died and now she would have to have Mr. Jarvis for a new father.

It was hard to put it out of her mind as she went downstairs. In the kitchen her mother was stirring batter in a bowl. "Corn bread tonight," she said cheerfully, and then paused as she saw Dorrie's face. "What's the matter, honey?"

"Mom, Erin's mother is going to marry this man — and Erin doesn't like him, he isn't nice. He doesn't really like Erin. He tried to lose her at the zoo. And if he married her mom maybe he'd keep on doing mean things like that — maybe worse things."

Mrs. Foster tried to understand all this. She had been thinking about dinner, and here suddenly was Dorrie all upset about Erin.

She stopped stirring the corn bread batter.

"I know you've been getting letters from Erin,"

she said. "I thought she was happy in her new home."

"She *was* happy. But now her mother wants to marry this Mr. Jarvis, and Erin doesn't *like* him."

Mrs. Foster shook her head. "It's not unusual for children not to want a parent to remarry. It's not unusual for Erin to want her mother all to herself just now and to resent someone trying to take her father's place. It's a natural reaction."

"But she doesn't *like* him, Mom. And he doesn't like her."

"That's probably just her imagination," Mrs. Foster said. She began to stir her batter again. "They'll probably get along fine when it comes down to it."

"Do you think so?" Dorrie asked.

"Of course. A lot of children whose parents remarry feel like that at first, but it works out. You'll see."

"I suppose so," Dorrie said. But she didn't really feel sure.

She carried plates and silverware into the dining room to set the table for dinner. Stevie had set up his Christmas-gift dominoes in a row at one end of the table. When he saw Dorrie coming with her plates and silverware he shouted, "Hey, Dorrie, watch this — total destruction!"

He flicked the first domino and it fell back against the second. The second fell against the third, the third fell against the fourth, and the whole long row, one by one, clattered down to the table.

Up in her room, before bedtime, Dorrie read Erin's letter a second time. The cold afternoon at the zoo . . . lunch with Aunt Margaret. Erin's panic at the zoo, her fear of the future, were all there in the letter.

Dear Erin, Dorrie began a letter of her own. *My mom says lots of kids feel the way you do.* . . .

She hoped what she was writing was true, and that things would work out when Erin's mother married Mr. Jarvis.

But part of her wished Mr. Jarvis would just go away and leave Erin and her mother alone.

12

But there was no chance of Mr. Jarvis going away.

It seemed to Erin he only came more and more as the early days of February went by. He came for dinner. He took Erin's mother out to dinner. One night he brought Aunt Margaret flowers and Erin a box of chocolates. He even brought a bouquet for Mrs. Higgins.

"Because you are such a superb cook," he told her. He stood in the kitchen doorway and produced the flowers from behind his back with a flourish, like a magician pulling flowers from his coat sleeve.

Mrs. Higgins bustled around, more eager than ever after that to make an extra good dinner for Mr. Jarvis. Erin didn't even want to eat the meal. "You're just waiting to get at the chocolates," Aunt Margaret teased her.

"But don't eat too many," she whispered, when she had a moment alone with Erin. "Mr. Jarvis meant well, but candy is bad for the teeth."

Erin stared at the chocolates, nestled in individual paper cups. "He probably wants me to eat them and have all my teeth fall out," she mumbled. Aunt Margaret didn't hear.

Erin made up her mind not to eat any — not even one. She offered the box after dinner in the living room, and when everyone (except Erin) took a piece, she sneaked off to the kitchen and gave the rest to Mrs. Higgins.

"Don't you want them?" Mrs. Higgins asked with surprise.

"My stomach doesn't feel good," Erin said. She kept her fingers crossed, hidden in her skirt.

"It doesn't?" Mrs. Higgins peered at her with concern.

"Oh, it's not bad," Erin said quickly. "Don't tell my mother. She'd just worry."

Mrs. Higgins took the box of chocolates home to her husband. No one ever asked Erin what happened to the candy. Aunt Margaret forgot about it, and Erin's mother was too busy going out with Mr. Jarvis to think about a box of chocolates.

However, Mrs. Lang did call Erin into her room one evening when she was dressing to go to dinner with Mr. Jarvis. A sleety rain that had been falling earlier had stopped and the air had a misty chill, haloing the street lamps and blurring the houses along the street.

It was one of Aunt Margaret's bridge nights and a friend had already come by to pick her up. Mrs. Higgins had gone home.

"Erin, I'm not quite ready," her mother said. "Will you go downstairs and let Mr. Jarvis in? He should be here any minute. Tell him I won't be long."

There was a scent of perfume in the bedroom. A blue dress lay across the bed. There were earrings and a bracelet on the dressing table.

Erin stood stubbornly by the bed, fingering the ruffle on the sleeve of the dress.

"Erin?"

"Do I have to?"

"He'll be here any minute and I'm not dressed yet."

"What will I say to him?"

She couldn't go downstairs and talk to Mr. Jarvis alone. Why wasn't her mother ready!

Mrs. Lang got up from the dressing table and took Erin gently by the shoulders. "Silly," she said, "you'll think of lots to talk about." She steered Erin toward the doorway just as the sound of the doorbell came from below.

"There he is now. Go along, Erin. Tell him I'll be down in a few minutes. It will be good for you two to talk together. I want you to be friends."

There was nothing Erin could do except go downstairs.

But her footsteps lagged on the stairs. The doorbell rang again.

"I'm coming, I'm coming," she muttered to herself. "Can't you wait a minute?"

When she opened the front door, Mr. Jarvis stood there in the misty night. He came in bringing the dampness and cold. "Hello there, Erin," he said cheerfully.

As though he really likes me, Erin thought.

"My mom's not ready yet."

Mr. Jarvis smiled faintly. Erin could tell he wasn't any happier to be alone with her than she was to be with him.

"Well, that's all right," he said. "You and I can have a little chat while we wait for her."

He left his coat in the entry and made himself at home in the living room.

There was no fire in the fireplace that night, and he stood by the hearth thoughtfully.

"This room was so warm and beautiful at Christmas, wasn't it, Erin. With the tree and the fire."

"Yeah . . . I guess."

"It was a nice Christmas. Did you get all the things you wanted?"

"No, I didn't," Erin said. "I wanted a kitten or a puppy."

She didn't really want to confide in Mr. Jarvis, but she had to say something. She wished her mother would come downstairs.

"Pets are nice." Mr. Jarvis nodded. "When your father and I were in Australia we had a pet koala bear. They're wild, you know. We'd leave out a pan of milk and some crusts of bread, bits of carrots — you know, odd things like that. And it came to our tents every night to eat. We called it Beggar. It got quite friendly . . . ah, here's your mother."

Mrs. Lang came into the room. The blue dress swirled softly as she walked.

"Aunt Margaret will be home before long," she said to Erin. "You'll be all right for a bit."

"I'm not a *child*," Erin said.

She didn't mean to sound cross. But she felt cross. She just wished Mr. Jarvis and her mother would go if they were going.

"Good-bye, sweetie." Her mother's kiss brushed Erin's cheek.

"Good-bye, beautiful." Mr. Jarvis waved his hand at Erin as he opened the front door and went out with her mother.

The door closed behind them, but Erin opened it just a crack and watched as they went down the walk and Mr. Jarvis opened the door of the car for her mother. The dome light went on in the car. Then the door closed and the light went out. Mr. Jarvis walked around the car and got in on the driver's side. Then they drove off into the misty night.

13

I know my mother only left us alone
on purpose. She wants us to be friends.

The word "friends" was underlined twice.
    Dorrie sat at the dining room table reading
the letter. She and Stevie were home alone, so
she had to do her homework downstairs. From
the living room she could hear the sound of the
television. The eight o'clock program was start-
ing.

She said she wasn't ready, but she
was just being slow on purpose. I
didn't know what to talk about. Mr.
Jarvis told me about the pet koala he
and my father had when they were in
Australia. They fed it scraps and
named it Beggar because it came
around every day for food.

72

There was more to the letter, but Dorrie kept reading the part about the pet koala.

She knew she had to write to Erin right away. Never mind stationery, that was way upstairs in her room. She took a sheet of notebook paper and began:

> *Dear Erin,*
> *Mr. Jarvis lied about having a pet koala. Koala bears live all their lives in trees — eucalyptus trees. I read that in a book. They get all their food from the leaves, and all the water they need, too. They sleep most of the time when they're not eating. A koala would never come down out of the tree begging food from people.*
> *I bet Mr. Jarvis wasn't ever even in Australia.*

Dorrie paused. If Mr. Jarvis hadn't been in Australia, why had he lied about it?

And if he hadn't been in Australia, did he even know Erin's father?

It was very puzzling. Mr. Jarvis must have known Erin's father, or how would he know about the trip to Australia?

And then Dorrie remembered Mr. Lang's book in the library. His picture had been on the back flap of the book jacket. There had been a long paragraph of information about him. She didn't remember all of it — something about where he had gone to college, and that he now taught English literature. She did remember there had been something about his love of traveling, beginning with a trip he took with some classmates to Australia during his college days.

Maybe Mr. Jarvis had seen that book, too, and read about Mr. Lang.

Dorrie didn't have all the answers, but she wanted Erin to know what she thought.

> *Maybe Mr. Jarvis didn't even know your dad. I don't think your mom would like him so much if she knew he lied about that. Tell her about the pet koala.*

There. Dorrie felt satisfied with the letter. Maybe Mrs. Lang wouldn't be getting married after all, and Erin wouldn't have to have Mr. Jarvis for a stepfather. Losing her in the zoo was a mean thing to do. And maybe he would go on doing even meaner things to Erin if he married her mother.

When Dorrie had the letter addressed, she went into the living room. Stevie was lying on his stomach in the middle of the floor, watching TV.

"Get your coat," Dorrie told him. "We have to go out."

Stevie looked up with surprise. "Out where?"

"I have to mail a letter."

"Mail a letter? Now?"

"Yes, now. Right now this minute." Dorrie was already putting on her coat. "Come on, Stevie. *Move.*"

"Can't I just wait here? You'll be right back."

"No, you can't just wait here. You know the rules."

The rules were: One, Dorrie would not leave Stevie alone in the house. Two, Stevie would obey Dorrie when she was in charge.

"I know, I know," Stevie complained. "If you leave me alone for one second the house will catch fire and burglars will kidnap me and — "

"Stevie, come *on!*" Dorrie wasn't even listening. While Stevie was still putting on his jacket she pushed him out the front door.

The mailbox was two blocks away. It stood at the corner of Cross Street and Elmwood Lane, brightly lighted by the corner street lamp.

"Why are we doing this?" Stevie protested. "Wait till I tell Mom. I'm missing my program."

"We're doing this because I want Erin to get this letter as fast as possible," Dorrie said. She shoved in the envelope and rattled the mailbox flap to be sure the letter went down. She felt thrilled with excitement to be dashing out into the night like this — and to be sending such important news to Erin.

75

Stevie pulled her back along the street impatiently, and she only vaguely noticed there was a drizzly rain falling.

Then, back home again, a terrible thought came to her: If Erin told her mother about the pet koala, Mr. Jarvis could just deny he had ever said such a thing. Erin's mother and Aunt Margaret would think Erin had made up the story because she didn't like Mr. Jarvis.

Now Dorrie wished she could get that letter back.

Leaving Stevie by the TV, Dorrie dashed upstairs to her room. Frantically she searched through her desk drawers for the first letter Erin had sent her. She was sure she still had it somewhere . . . on that first letter Erin had written her phone number. . . .

Yes! There was the letter, Erin's very first letter, telling about her new school and Aunt Margaret's house. Before Mr. Jarvis had ever come to their front door.

Dorrie dialed the number with such haste she misdialed a six instead of a seven and had to start all over.

When she heard the phone ringing at Erin's end, she closed her eyes and whispered, "Please be home, Erin. Please be home."

14

Erin was not only home, but she answered the phone herself.

"Will you get that, Erin," Aunt Margaret said when the phone rang. She was talking with Mr. Jarvis. Mr. Jarvis had come for dinner (again!) and they were all sitting in the living room.

The telephone was on a small table in the hallway between the living room and dining room. The last voice Erin expected to hear was Dorrie Foster's. She didn't even recognize it.

"Erin? Hi, this is me, Dorrie."

"Dorrie . . . Dorrie Foster?"

"Yes, me — listen Erin, I sent you a letter about the koala bear but now I've got a better idea."

Erin was confused, but before she could ask any questions, Dorrie rushed on.

"You said Mr. Jarvis told you he had a pet koala in Australia, but he was lying, Erin. Koalas live all their lives in eucalyptus trees. They eat the

77

leaves and sleep the rest of the time. They never come down out of their trees to get food. Mr. Jarvis lied. I bet he was never in Australia — maybe he never even knew your dad."

Erin was trying to understand. From the living room she could hear a murmur of voices. Her mother was laughing over something Mr. Jarvis said.

"He could have read about your dad going to Australia," Dorrie rushed on. "It's on his book cover. Anyway, in my letter I told you to tell your mom about the koala — but that won't do. She'll ask Mr. Jarvis why he told you he had a pet koala when koalas only live in trees — and then he'll say *you* made the whole thing up and he never said such a thing."

Dorrie paused for a breath.

"You've got to get Mr. Jarvis to tell your mother about the koala *himself*. Then you can tell her about koalas living in trees and she'll know Mr. Jarvis is lying."

"But he's in the pictures," Erin said.

The pictures of Australia. Dorrie had forgotten all about them. Her racing thoughts came to a stop.

"Dorrie? Are you still there?"

"Yes, I'm here," Dorrie said. "Oh, Erin, I don't *know*, but something's wrong somewhere. Get Mr. Jarvis to tell your mom about the koala and see what happens. Do it next time you see him."

"He's here now," Erin said.

"He is? Then do it now, Erin," Dorrie urged.

"I'll try." Erin didn't feel very confident. Mr. Jarvis always made her uncomfortable.

"Okay," Dorrie said. "Let me know what happens."

"I will. And thanks for calling."

Erin hung up the telephone. When Dorrie's voice was gone she realized how comforting it had been. Now she was all alone.

She stood for a few moments, feeling alone and wishing she was braver. How could she get Mr. Jarvis to talk about the koala? Could she just come right out and say, "Tell my mom about the pet koala you and my daddy had in Australia." That would be hard to do.

She went back into the living room slowly. A fire was burning in the fireplace. Aunt Margaret was just helping herself to salted nuts from a dish on the table by her chair. Mr. Jarvis was sitting by Erin's mother.

"Who was that, honey?" Erin's mother asked as Erin came into the room.

"Oh, it was Dorrie, a girl from back in Breming."

"How nice of her to call." Mrs. Lang was pleased that Erin's friends remembered her. "Isn't that the girl who's been writing to you?"

Erin nodded and stood by the fireside awkwardly.

And then Aunt Margaret said, continuing a story, "I think Lillian would be quite lost without her little dog. . . ."

Erin didn't know who Lillian was — probably one of Aunt Margaret's bridge-playing friends. It didn't matter. Lillian's little dog was Erin's chance.

"I wish I had a dog," she blurted out boldly.

"Darling, you know we talked about that — " her mother started to say. But Erin hurried on. "If Daddy was here, he'd let me have a dog — don't you think so, Mr. Jarvis? Daddy liked pets. Remember the koala bear you told me about?"

"Of course," Mr. Jarvis said. "Cutest little fellow you can imagine."

"A koala bear?" Aunt Margaret turned toward Mr. Jarvis.

"It was when we were in Australia," Mr. Jarvis explained. "We saved dinner scraps for it, a bit of milk. It came around every day. Got quite tame."

"That's not true," Erin said. Her voice was trembling. "Koalas live in trees."

"And they get all their nourishment from the leaves," Aunt Margaret spoke up. She was looking at Mr. Jarvis with a puzzled expression. "They never eat dinner scraps."

Help had come from an unexpected direction. Erin felt a flood of love for Aunt Margaret.

"Mr. Jarvis, if you were ever in Australia you

would know about koalas." Aunt Margaret was staring at him intently.

Erin's mother was startled and confused. "John. . . ?" She turned to him uncertainly.

"Yes, yes, of course I was in Australia." Mr. Jarvis tried to sound assured and cheerful. "You saw the pictures. Philip and I were friends, good friends."

But it didn't sound true.

Like Stevie Foster's row of dominoes, Mr. Jarvis' lies began to topple one by one.

15

Icicles were melting in the late February thaw when the next letter came from Erin. It was waiting for Dorrie when she came home from school, waiting for her on the hall table as the hours passed.

> Dear Dorrie,
> You were right. Mr. Jarvis was
> never in Australia with my father. He
> never even knew my father. He read
> about Mom and me moving to Ashford
> to live with Aunt Margaret, and then
> he read about Daddy on the book cover
> at the library.
> Aunt Margaret says Mr. Jarvis just
> needed money for his antique shop and
> figured Mom would have insurance
> money after Daddy died — and that
> Aunt Margaret had money.
> He thought if he said he knew

Daddy, my mom would like and trust him.

She did like him. I guess a lot. And I think she feels bad to think he could lie about everything like that. But she doesn't want to see him anymore.

He was nice to Aunt Margaret and Mom to get the money, but he didn't want to be bothered by having me around.

About the pictures. Aunt Margaret says that's easy. All the men had beards, and it was such a small photo you really couldn't tell who was who. It was twenty-five years ago, too.

Aunt Margaret says Mr. Jarvis was just lucky because one of the men was a little taller than the others, and Mr. Jarvis is tall. But she says it didn't matter if he looked like someone in the picture. He could always say he was the one who took the pictures.

She says he ought to know eucalyptus leaves aren't just for spicy air in antique shops.

I hope my mom does meet somebody nice someday. I guess I wouldn't mind that. I just don't want it to be someone mean like Mr. Jarvis.

We're going to stay here with Aunt

Margaret for a while. And that's okay
with me.

I have a new friend at school. Her
name is Margie. She lives on the next
block. We walk home together. Yesterday Mrs. Higgins let us make fudge in
the kitchen. Mrs. Higgins is very
happy because her horoscope has been
good. My mom still says not to believe
too much in that.

Thanks for everything, Dorrie.
Write soon.

Love, Erin

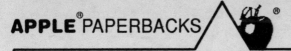

APPLE® PAPERBACKS

Pick an Apple and Polish Off Some Great Reading!

BEST-SELLING APPLE TITLES

❏ MT43944-8	**Afternoon of the Elves** Janet Taylor Lisle	**$2.75**
❏ MT43109-9	**Boys Are Yucko** Anna Grossnickle Hines	**$2.95**
❏ MT43473-X	**The Broccoli Tapes** Jan Slepian	**$2.95**
❏ MT42709-1	**Christina's Ghost** Betty Ren Wright	**$2.75**
❏ MT43461-6	**The Dollhouse Murders** Betty Ren Wright	**$2.75**
❏ MT43444-6	**Ghosts Beneath Our Feet** Betty Ren Wright	**$2.75**
❏ MT44351-8	**Help! I'm a Prisoner in the Library** Eth Clifford	**$2.95**
❏ MT44567-7	**Leah's Song** Eth Clifford	**$2.75**
❏ MT43618-X	**Me and Katie (The Pest)** Ann M. Martin	**$2.95**
❏ MT41529-8	**My Sister, The Creep** Candice F. Ransom	**$2.75**
❏ MT46075-7	**Sixth Grade Secrets** Louis Sachar	**$2.95**
❏ MT42882-9	**Sixth Grade Sleepover** Eve Bunting	**$2.95**
❏ MT41732-0	**Too Many Murphys** Colleen O'Shaughnessy McKenna	**$2.75**

Available wherever you buy books, or use this order form.

Scholastic Inc., P.O. Box 7502, 2931 East McCarty Street, Jefferson City, MO 65102

Please send me the books I have checked above. I am enclosing $_____ (please add $2.00 to cover shipping and handling). Send check or money order — no cash or C.O.D.s please.

Name _____

Address _____

City_____ State/Zip _____

Please allow four to six weeks for delivery. Offer good in the U.S.A. only. Sorry, mail orders are not available to residents of Canada. Prices subject to change.

APP1192